BERNARD'S GANG

Everyone but Bernard seems to have a friend – and right now, he really needs one. In fact, he could do with a whole army of them!

Dick Cate was born in Ferryhill, County Durham. He was a teacher, for many years, at various schools around the country until his retirement in 1982. His first book for children, *On the Run*, was published in 1973. Since then he has written many titles, some of which feature the character Billy Robinson. These include *Old Dog, New Tricks* (Winner of the 1979 Other Award), *Ghost Dog* and *Fibs* (shortlisted for the 1991 Guardian Fiction Award). For Walker, he has written *Rodney Penfold, Genius* and *The Doomsday Diary of Ermengarde Hulke*. *Bernard's Gang* is Dick Cate's third story about Bernard, the others being *Bernard's Prize* and *Bernard's Magic*, which was shortlisted for the Nassen Special Educational Awards Children's Book of the Year. Married, with four grown-up children and five grandchildren, four grandsons and a granddaughter, Dick Cate lives in Huddersfield.

Bernard's Gang

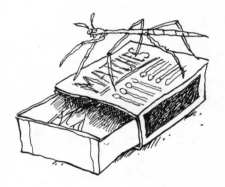

DICK CATE

Illustrations by
SCOULAR ANDERSON

WALKER BOOKS
AND SUBSIDIARIES
LONDON • BOSTON • SYDNEY

For Nat

.

First published 1998 by Walker Books Ltd
87 Vauxhall Walk, London SE11 5HJ

This edition published 1998

2 4 6 8 10 9 7 5 3 1

Text © 1998 Dick Cate
Illustrations © 1998 Scoular Anderson

The right of Dick Cate to be identified as author of
this work has been asserted by him in accordance with the
Copyright, Designs and Patents Act 1988.

This book has been typeset in Plantin.

Printed in England

British Library Cataloguing in Publication Data
A catalogue record for this book is available
from the British Library.

ISBN 0-7445-6032-2

Contents

Chapter 1

One Friday afternoon Bernard was standing in the middle of the playground surrounded by people having fun and not one person asked him to join in.

Of course, he knew why. If he played chasey he kept having to stop to use his inhaler. And if *he* stopped, of course everybody else had to stop. And people didn't like that.

It was worse if he played football. Every time he kicked a ball it somehow went the wrong way. When people were choosing sides he was always the last one to be picked. Last week the side that got him gave him away to the other side for nothing: they called it a free transfer.

Not that he was any worse than Squashy Petch, who was playing football down at the bottom of the yard with Ozzie Flatt and his pals.

Until yesterday Bernard and Squashy had been special friends. They were going to call themselves The Pear Gang because there were only two of them, and they'd decided to invent a secret code. So far, they'd worked out three words:

doog = good   *nodrap* = pardon
oireech = cheerio

They were going to have badges the shape of pears and everybody would be baffled because they wouldn't know that a pair meant two. To be honest, Bernard hadn't known until Squashy told him. Squashy was pretty smart. He was on Purple Level Five of the Literary Treasure Chest. Last night Bernard had cut out the badges from a cornflake packet. Now, he supposed it would all be a waste of time because this morning Squashy seemed to be special friends with Ozzie Flatt instead.

Once Bernard had been pals with Ozzie himself. But being pals with Ozzie had proved to be a high-risk occupation. Bernard had found he wasn't cut out for it, not on a daily basis.

Down at the bottom of the yard Ozzie sent three people flying as he dribbled the ball, shot from two metres, missed by a mile and shouted, "GOAL!"

Bernard could not understand how he'd ever been friends with such a person. Ozzie had this enormous rat called Oscar that he kept down his trousers. He kept taking Oscar out and frightening people. He always had this loopy grin on his face. Everybody knew he wasn't very bright. Bernard might not exactly be brilliant but Ozzie Flatt hadn't even *started* on the Literary Treasure Chest. Louise Bruce, who Bernard liked because she was kind to people, helped him to read baby books.

Now he was slapping hands with everybody, his latest craze. When he slapped Squashy's hand there was a terrific *crack!* and Bernard could just imagine how much it must hurt. Even from this distance he could see Squashy trying not to yelp. Not that Bernard really cared. He had only been pals with Squashy because nobody else liked him.

A great cheer came from the bottom of the yard. Ozzie was trying to push Squashy up to the top of the school wall. There was a drop on the other side that could cause a person to end up on hospital food for a fortnight. Not that Ozzie would manage. He might be strong but it would take at least *three* people to raise Squashy that high.

"Hi, Bernard!" It was Louise Bruce. "Looking forward to Monday?"

Next week Miss Trim wanted them to bring their pets to school and they were all going to think very deeply about animals.

"Not really," said Bernard.

"Why not?"

"I haven't got a pet."

"What about your Cheri?"

Cheri was their overweight dachshund.

"Cheri's really my mum's dog," said Bernard, "and she's got a poorly leg. I used to have a pet of my own once. A hamster called Emily Poot."

"What a lovely name."

"But she's dead now."

"How sad!"

"Buried under a tree at my dad's house, where we used to live."

"I'm so sorry," Louise said sympathetically.

She was a very sympathetic person. Her sympathy, and the thought of poor dead Emily, made tears start prickling round Bernard's eyes and – quite naturally – he didn't want a girl to see him cry so he said, "Sorry, Louise, got to go somewhere fast."

And he headed for the bogs.

Chapter 2

Bernard was drying his hands when a big boy called Baxter came in.

Bernard had heard things about Baxter. But he wasn't too worried at first because Baxter smiled at him.

Through a mirror Bernard watched Baxter push open all the cubicle doors and look in. Bernard didn't know why he did that but it was still OK.

Then Baxter came up to Bernard and said, "Aren't you that kid who's always poorly?"

"Yes," said Bernard, smiling. It was nice to be recognized.

"What's your name again?"

"Bernard," said Bernard.

"Nice name. How you doing, Bernard?"

"OK."

Bernard started to walk away but Baxter caught his arm.

"Where you going?"

"Nowhere."

"Maybe we could have a chat. Right now I'm a bit short of money."

Bernard knew the feeling. He was short of money himself. As far as he could remember he had been short of money ever since they left his dad.

"I'm saving up for a new bike," Baxter told him.

"So am I!" said Bernard. It seemed an amazing coincidence.

"How much you got?" asked Baxter.

"Nearly fifteen pounds."

"You must be rich in your family."

"We're not," said Bernard. "My mum has hardly any money at all."

"Don't you live with your dad?"

"They split up."

"Hard cheese. Maybe you could lend me some?"

Bernard wasn't so sure.

"How much you got on you now?"

Bernard wasn't even sure about that.

"Empty your pockets out. Let's see how much."

Bernard took all the money out of his

pockets and handed it to Baxter, who counted it.

"Not a lot," said Baxter, laughing, as if it was a joke. "I make it twenty-seven p. Want to check that, Bernard?"

Bernard shook his head.

"Tell you what, write it down, Bernard. You *can* write, can you?"

Bernard nodded. He wasn't particularly good at it but at least he *could* write. Not like Ozzie Flatt.

At that moment the door opened and another big boy came in. He winked at Baxter, then stepped up to the urinal. Baxter went to the paper-towel dispenser and started drying his hands. He hadn't even washed them yet.

Then the headmaster, Mr Fearby, came in.

"Everything all right, boys?" he asked.

"Fine, sir," said Baxter. "Just drying my hands."

"Good boy. You all right, Bernard?"

"Yes, sir," Bernard said.

"Jolly good, don't be late for lessons, boys."

"No, sir."

Mr Fearby went out.

"Tell you what, Bernard," said Baxter, throwing his paper towel at him so that it bounced off his chest. "I'd like two quid from you on Monday morning. Just for a lend, of course." The other big boy seemed to think that was funny. "All right?"

"OK," said Bernard. Then he remembered. "Sorry, Baxter, I won't be at school on Monday morning," he said. "I've got to go to hospital to see Dr Tom."

"Dr Tom?"

"He's a head-shrink," said the other boy, laughing.

"Is he, Bernard? Is Dr Tom a head-shrink?"

Bernard didn't know what a head-shrink was.

"You in the loony bin now, Bernard?"

"I usually just see him in the morning – for a talk."

"Told you!" said the other big boy.

"No problem," said Baxter. "See you in here straight after dinner?"

"OK," said Bernard.

"And, Bernard, I want to show you something." Baxter walked to the cubicles and pulled one of the doors towards him. "Watch this." He punched his fist forward. There was a *wham!* and the cubicle door slammed back against the cubicle wall with a *crash!* The other big boy laughed.

"And this is the funny thing," said Baxter. He held out his fist. Not a mark on it. "That's because I do karate," he said. "Amazing how it toughens the knuckles! Don't forget my two quid, will you, Bernard?"

He smiled as he went out.

Chapter 3

Bernard didn't tell his mum about Baxter. He knew what would happen if he did. She would go straight up to school and tell Mr Fearby. Then what?

In any case, it was the wrong time to worry her. She always worried when Bernard's dad came to "borrow" him for the day. And he was coming tomorrow.

He didn't tell Tony either. Tony and his mum had been going out together for two weeks now and Bernard suspected they were in love because last night they were drinking out of the same glass.

Tony was up in the bathroom now, mending a dripping tap that had been driving Bernard's mum crazy since they moved here. At teatime she had asked Tony if he knew how to mend a tap.

"No," he'd said, "but I know a man who does."

After tea he'd gone to the library and borrowed a book about mending things.

After supper he'd studied it and said,

"Got such a thing as an adjustable spanner?" and Bernard's mum had said, "No, but I've got a pair of nail scissors."

So he'd gone round to next door and come back with a whopping big spanner over his shoulder. "Anybody fancy their teeth adjusting?" he'd asked before going upstairs.

After he had helped to put away the supper things Bernard spread some newspaper on the table and started painting. He concentrated hard, hoping it would help him forget Baxter but the thought kept bobbling up in his mind.

Miss Trim was forever sticking Bernard's paintings on the wall. It was embarrassing, really, but he liked it. Now, though, he hardly knew what he was doing until his mum said, "What are you doing, Bernard?"

Actually, he was painting the two Pear Gang badges he'd cut out last night. He'd just finished them. He knew they were a waste of time.

His mum came over to have a look.

"They're lovely, Bernard," she said. "What are they for?"

"Nothing," he said.

"Why pears?"

He shrugged.

"Is something the matter?"

"No."

"Why don't you go and play outside with your friends?"

"I haven't got any friends."

"What about Squashy?"

"He's friends with somebody else now."

"Well, what about Ozzie Flatt?"

"That's who he's friends with."

"Are you worried about tomorrow? About Dad?"

"No."

"There's no need to be," she said.

"I'm not worried."

"You might enjoy it this time," she said.

He'd thought he'd enjoy it last time. He *always* thought he'd enjoy it. But somehow he never did. Something always went wrong. And he didn't like Debbs, who lived at his dad's house now. Debbs didn't like being called Aunty – she said she wasn't old enough. She pretended to like Bernard but he knew she didn't. Last time she didn't want him to have a look at Emily Poot's grave and got upset when he walked some soil on to her carpet.

"I might get my bike this time," he said.

"You might."

His dad still had his old bike. His mum had bought him another but it was a second-hand knack and the handlebars were wobbly.

"If I had my old bike I know I could ride no-handed."

"It would be too small for you now, Bernard."

"I'm the only one in our class who can't ride no-handed."

"What about Squashy?"

"He did it the other night in the park."

"Maybe he'll show you how."

"He hates me. I'll never be able to ride

no-handed! I'll be the only one in the whole school!"

They both suddenly realized Tony was watching them from the doorway.

"Time for a demo, folks?"

They followed him upstairs and into the bathroom. He pointed at the tap and said, *"Da-daaa!"*

It was true. For the first time in history the tap wasn't dripping. Tony turned it on: water gushed out. He turned it off: the water stopped.

"No more drips!" he said.

"Except for me!" said Bernard's mum.

They both saw she was crying.

Chapter 4

As usual his mum didn't come out to say hello to his dad when he arrived.

She opened the front door for Bernard. "Remember to take your shoes off straight away," she said. "And this time don't be cheeky to Debbs."

She stayed by the door while he walked down the garden path and she didn't speak until he reached the gate. Then she called out, "Any idea what time you'll be bringing him back?"

His dad didn't answer. He must have heard, though, even above the noise from his radio. As Bernard reached the car his dad leaned over and shoved the door open for him.

"Brought some slippers this time, Dad," Bernard told him.

"Wonderful news! Get in and belt up, son."

He leaned over again and pulled Bernard's door shut, then looked at Bernard's mum still standing by the door. Looked at her hard. Then he turned up the radio even louder and drove off fast.

Bernard's dad liked putting his foot down. Every time they went round corners his tyres screeched. Bernard's mum used to hate it when he drove like that. She would keep asking him to slow down but he just went faster.

"Well?" his dad shouted over the radio. "What's he like? Your mother's new boyfriend!"

Bernard hadn't a clue what to say. His mum hadn't told him to say nothing about Tony. But he knew he shouldn't.

"I know all about him, anyhow," his dad said, looking down at him. "You'd be surprised at what I know. His name's Tony, isn't it?"

Bernard nodded.

"Fancies himself, does he?"

Bernard shrugged.

"Bet he isn't as tough as me!"

He probably wasn't. His dad was a pretty tough guy. If they had a fight his dad would probably win. He was bigger than Tony.

"There's a tough guy at our school, Dad,"

said Bernard.

His dad pulled on to the motorway and straight into the fast lane.

"What about him?"

"He just keeps shoving me around."

"So what you going to do about it?"

"I don't know."

"You want my advice? Hit him where it hurts!"

Bernard wasn't exactly sure where that was. And even if he'd known, he wasn't sure he'd have wanted to hit Baxter there because there was a possibility that Baxter might hit him back and if he did it wouldn't be good news – Bernard suspected he felt pain a lot more than other kids (about twice as much).

"My advice is don't take any sass, kid," said his dad. "Learn to stand up for yourself. I always did when I was a kid and it never did me any harm. The trouble is, your mother's mollycoddled you. She always did. I tried to stop her when we were together but she wouldn't take any notice of me. Your mother hasn't the first idea. You have to stand on your own two feet in this world, Bernard. What do you think of the new car?"

"Which new car, Dad?"

"This one! *This one!*" He banged his hands up and down on the steering wheel. "What exactly is the matter with you, son?"

"It's OK," said Bernard, trying to look impressed.

"OK?"

"It's good," said Bernard, trying to look a lot more impressed.

But his dad didn't believe him. He leaned forward and turned up the radio even more. "I'll show you how good it is, Bernard! Give it some wellie, shall we?" And his foot went down.

Chapter 5

Debbs was in the front garden when they arrived. She always wore a funny hat and gloves when she did the garden.

"I thought I'd just get a bit done before it rains again," she said.

"Good idea!" said Bernard's dad.

"We might as well go in for lunch," Debbs said.

She always called it that.

"Good idea!" said Bernard's dad.

Bernard changed into his slippers as soon as he went in the hall and hung up his coat straight away.

"Thank you!" said Debbs.

"Good boy," said his dad.

"Would you like to wash hands?" asked Debbs.

"Can he just do it in the kitchen?" asked his dad.

"I suppose so," said Debbs.

So Bernard padded into the kitchen to wash his hands, even though they were perfectly clean. When he'd dried them he went into the room that Debbs now called The Diner and was just about to slide back the patio door so that he could have a quick look at Emily Poot's grave when he heard Debbs behind him say, "Would you like to sit up now, Bernard? It's rude to keep people waiting."

The table was neatly set out with pink serviettes, glasses for the grown-ups, a plastic cup for Bernard. Debbs always gave him a plastic cup.

It was always dead quiet when they ate at his dad's house now because Debbs believed everybody should chew nicely with their mouth shut. But just to make polite conversation, Bernard mentioned the fact that he was now finally on Yellow Level of the Literary Treasure Chest. He thought they might be interested but all Debbs said was, "Is something wrong with that cabbage?"

"Eat it up," said his dad. "There's a good lad."

"It was the same last time!" said Debbs.

"Have a bit of patience, Debbs," said his dad.

The fact was Bernard hated cabbage. But it wasn't only that which made him decide to be cheeky. Somehow Debbs always upset him inside, the same as cabbage did, really, only worse.

"Can I can go to see Emily Poot's grave after?" he asked.

Debbs stopped a forkful of something halfway to her mouth. "Emily is dead, Bernard," she told him. "Nothing we can do will change that."

"I just wanted to say goodbye."

"I seem to remember you did that last time, when you walked soil in all over my carpet."

"I just want to say goodbye again."

"I can't honestly see the point. In any case, I don't think we really know where she is any longer. I've put in a host of new plants."

"*And* you've shifted things around a lot," said his dad.

Bernard looked at the patio door. "I won't walk on the soil."

"It's the lawn I'm frightened of," said Debbs.

"We've no idea where she is, son. Honestly."

"*I* know where she is," said Bernard.

"You don't, Bernard," said Debbs, laying down her fork. "You *think* you know but you don't." She looked at Bernard's dad. "And what about that blessed bike?" she asked.

"Blessed bike?"

"You know very well what blessed bike! Why don't you give him the blessed bike and have done with it?"

Bernard's dad looked at Debbs in the same hard way that he'd looked at Bernard's mum. They stared at each other. It was like a fight. After a bit they both went back to eating. But Bernard knew he would never see his bike again.

After they'd cleared the table Bernard asked

to go to the toilet. He didn't really want to go but from the upstairs landing window he would be able to see Emily's grave. If need be he would say goodbye from there. He felt sure she would understand.

Once in the toilet he slid the bolt. The plastic shelves where his dad used to keep his shaving stuff had gone. His mum used to use his razor to shave off what she called her little whiskers. After a while Bernard pulled the chain so they would hear downstairs. Then he undid the bolt and tiptoed along the landing.

He hardly recognized the garden. Where the path had been there wasn't one, but there were paths everywhere else. The worst thing was, the tree Emily was buried under didn't seem to be there any more. And because the garden was so changed he wasn't sure where the tree used to be. He looked and looked but in the end he gave up. He had the feeling he would never find Emily's grave, just like he'd never see his bike again.

He leaned close to the window and said, *"I just want to say, Emily, that I'll never forget you."* But he had no sense of her hearing him. None at all.

"What on earth are you doing up there?" he heard Debbs shout.

"Nothing," said Bernard.

"What's he up to?" asked his dad.

"You know very well what he's up to!"

"Come down, son! Come on! I've got a treat for you today. Know where we're going? Dark Wood."

Bernard liked Dark Wood. When his mum and dad were together they all used to go there to watch the rabbits playing.

"There's a car rally on," said his dad. "Great, eh?"

Bernard tried not to look too disappointed.

Chapter 6

Debbs didn't come with them. She had to get her hair done.

The rain started just after they got to Dark Wood. The drips kept going down Bernard's neck. He didn't like the way the cars were tearing up the ground. He kept thinking of the poor rabbits.

He tried to look interested, for his dad's sake. But he can't have succeeded because after the second race his dad said, "I get the feeling you're not enjoying this, son?"

"I am, Dad."

"There's no need to lie!" his dad said. "You're not talking to your mother now. If there's one thing I can't stand it's a liar!"

"I *am* enjoying it," said Bernard. "Honestly."

Shortly after that, they left.

"Take it!" his dad said as they left the motorway.

He thrust a twenty pound note at Bernard. "What is it?"

"You know very well what it is!"

The funny thing was, Bernard really didn't want to take it. Normally, he was glad when people gave him money. But this time was different.

"Take it!" his dad said angrily.

So Bernard took it. He was scared that if he didn't his dad would get even angrier and drive even faster.

They didn't speak again for the rest of the journey.

And although his dad had the radio on very loud it seemed to Bernard that a great silence gradually filled the car. A silence that seemed to grow bigger the further they went.

And out of the silence a question arose in Bernard's mind. A really scary question: *What if his dad didn't love him any more?*

And out of that question an even scarier question came: *If your own dad didn't love you, who did?*

In a way, that was worse than the idea of

Baxter waiting for him in the bogs after dinner on Monday.

Chapter 7

"Of course he still loves you!" his mum said when he told her. "Whatever makes you say a thing like that?"

Bernard told her about the long silence in the car.

"Your dad always finds it hard to say what he means. He always did."

"I don't want this, either," Bernard said, taking the twenty pound note from his pocket and placing it on the kitchen table.

His mum looked at him.

"Please take it, Bernard," she said.

"I don't want it."

"Put it in your money box. It'll come in handy."

It occurred to Bernard that he could use the money to give to Baxter. But he still didn't take it back.

"If you say no to a present," his mum said, "you might hurt the person who's giving it to you. You wouldn't want that?"

Bernard wasn't sure.

"Please, Bernard."

Bernard reached out and put the note in his pocket again.

"She didn't want me to see Emily Poot's grave, either," he said.

"Don't call her *she*, Bernard. And I'm sure that's not true."

He told his mum what had happened. Standing on the landing and not being able to find Emily's grave because the tree had gone.

"She wouldn't even let me go outside."

"She probably didn't want you to get wet."

"I only wanted to say goodbye."

"I know that, Bernard. But does it really matter? I mean, is it really important?"

Bernard couldn't quite understand what his mum was trying to say. He pulled himself back slightly to get a better look at her.

"I mean, it's just Emily's body, isn't it?" she said. "And her body isn't the important thing any more."

"What is the important thing?"

"Her spirit, I suppose," his mum said.

Bernard looked at her harder. "Where exactly is her spirit?" he asked.

"I'm not sure, Bernard. I suppose it's all around us."

Bernard looked all round the kitchen.

"Is it here now?"

"It could be."

"I can't see it."

"You can't see spirit, Bernard. But you might feel its presence."

He couldn't feel Emily's presence. But for some reason Bernard felt better. He didn't want his mum to know that though.

"He wouldn't give me my bike, either."

"We've been over all this before, Bernard. It's two years since we left your dad. You've grown."

"He could still let me try it."

"It would be a waste of time."

"I don't think he even has it. I think he's taken it to a car-boot."

"What makes you think that?" said his mum.

He told her about Debbs wanting him to get it down from the garage loft and his dad's hard look.

"He's still got it, Bernard," his mum said. "Don't you worry!"

"Then why doesn't he let me have it?"

"Don't you know, Bernard? The reason is he wants you to come back to him. That's what he's really hoping."

Bernard looked at her. "With you, you mean?"

"Maybe. I don't know."

"But you don't want to?"

"No. I don't."

"Why not?"

She paused. "Because I'm happier as we are. Aren't you?"

It was true. She *was* happier. Even though their house was small and scratty and they couldn't afford things. And he was happier himself. Though he wasn't ready to admit that.

"If I had my old bike I bet I could ride with

no hands," he said.

"I nearly forgot," said his mum. "Tony's stopped your handlebars wobbling with that big spanner thing. We'll go down the park tomorrow."

Chapter 8

Dr Tom was wearing a Mickey Mouse T-shirt when Bernard went to see him on Monday morning. He was sitting on a window-ledge looking down into the big hole that the hospital was built round. There was a pong of dinners cooking and the clatter of dishes.

"Hi, Bernard," said Dr Tom when he came in. "Pull up a pew."

Bernard sat down.

"How's tricks?"

"Fine."

"Nice weekend?"

"I rode my bike with no hands on Sunday."

"I've never seen a bike with no hands," said Dr Tom. He waited till Bernard smiled. "So you finally made it. How come? You get a new bike?"

Bernard shook his head.

"Tony fixed my handlebars."

"Tony?"

"My mum's new boyfriend. I rode all the way from the tennis courts to the swings with no hands."

"I've never seen swings with no hands either."

"I never fell off once," said Bernard.

"Talking of which, Bernard, in our previous ramblings, I think you mentioned a friend by the name of Squashy Petch?"

"What about him?"

"He's just fallen off something and broken his ankle. He's had a cast put on. I said you might wander into the Children's Ward and say hello before you go to school."

Bernard tried to look pleased. Normally he liked cheering people up. But the only black spot in the park yesterday had been seeing Squashy and Ozzie having fun together.

"That is OK, Bernard?" Dr Tom asked.

"We're not really friends now."

"That's funny. When I mentioned your name he seemed pleased."

"Did he?"

"He did indeed. So perhaps you'd think of calling in to see him anyhow. Just to cheer him up. OK?"

Bernard thought about it for a moment and then said, "OK."

"And how was Saturday? I believe you went to your dad's again? How did things go this time? Want to talk about it?"

Bernard didn't. Not really. But bit by bit he started telling Dr Tom, and Dr Tom listened quietly. He was the best listener Bernard knew. And when Bernard had finished he said, "I wonder why you didn't want to take the money, Bernard."

"I don't know."

"Twenty pounds is a lot."

"I know."

"How did you get on with Dad this time?"

"OK."

His eyes started to prickle.

Dr Tom passed him a tissue and said, "Have a good blow."

Bernard had two good blows. When the tears had almost stopped he managed to say, "I don't think my dad likes me any more."

"I think you're wrong, Bernard. I'm sure

your dad likes you. You know, you're very likeable, really. What does your mum say about this?"

"She says Dad doesn't always say what he means."

"I think your mum's right. A lot of people don't say what they mean. Or can't. But anyway, what *I'm* trying to say is, you're a really nice kid. Why else was Squashy Petch – your so-called ex-friend – so keen to see you this morning? I'm not just saying that because I'm your doctor, Bernard. You really are one of the all-time goodies. In fact, I've just thought of a brilliant idea. Say it aloud, Bernard. Say, 'I'm an all-time goody.'"

"I'm an all-time goody," said Bernard, smiling.

"Only smile when I crack a joke, Bernard, OK? It might be a good idea to repeat it to yourself now and then. Why are you smiling, Bernard? Please don't smile. Say it every time you blink or blow your nose. You never know, it might do some good."

Dr Tom leaned back for a moment before going on.

"I don't know if you've noticed it before, Bernard, but parents are very like carrots. Have you ever noticed that? Some are smart carrots – like your mum. Others are not so smart. You could call these others slow-learning carrots. The point is, there are no two carrots alike. Have you ever seen two carrots the same?"

"No," said Bernard, smiling again.

"There you are then. That proves I'm right. Anything else bothering you? Everything OK at school?"

"Fine," said Bernard. Then after a moment he said no and told Dr Tom about Baxter.

"Will Baxter be at school this morning?" Dr Tom asked.

"I think so."

"Have you brought the two pounds?"

Bernard nodded.

"That's good. You know why? Because it leaves you with two options. Which is always good. But answer me this, Bernard. What do you think will happen if you give Baxter the money?"

"He might ask for more?"

"I'd bet on it, Bernard. And I'm not a betting man. I'd risk really serious money on it. Maybe twenty pence. Please don't smile when I'm trying to be serious. The point is this. When he comes at you for the money you can either hand it over or not. It's up to you. Hand it over or say no and stick it out. Do you think you can stick it out?"

Bernard shrugged.

"I'd like you to. I'd like you to say no. But if you can't, don't worry about it. It's nothing to be ashamed of. You know why a lot of big boys are called big, Bernard? It's because they are big. But at least you can try to say no. There's an old saying, Bernard: The longest journey in the world starts with one small step. It's supposed to be a Chinese saying but a guy from Oldham told me. Not that it matters. The main thing is, it's true, whether you're in Oldham or China. Do you think you can take one small step?"

"I'll try."

"Good lad. And if you do hand over the money, then I think it's time to call in the cavalry. I mean, tell Miss Trim. Or your mum. Or Tony. Otherwise, you can kiss goodbye to that new bike."

Bernard looked up at him.

"I don't need a new bike now Tony's mended my old one."

"I'd forgotten about that. You're quite right, Bernard."

"Tonight we're going down to the park again to see if I can ride all the way round the tennis courts with no hands."

"I've never seen a tennis court with no hands, Bernard."

"And if I do, Tony's going to take us all to the Taj Mahal for a treat."

"You know what I think about Tony?" Dr Tom said. "In my opinion he's a very smart carrot indeed!"

Chapter 9

As Bernard went into the Children's Ward the nurse at reception said, "Bernard! How nice to see you again!" and another nurse said, "Ah! My favourite patient!"

Bernard had forgotten all about them but now he remembered that they'd looked after him when he'd been in for his operation.

He soon saw Squashy at the far end looking sorry for himself.

"Hi!" said Bernard when he reached his bed. "OK?"

"Fine," said Squashy. "I just broke my ankle, that's all. Want to sign my pot?" He handed Bernard a pen, clicking it so it was ready to write. "You'll be Numero Uno."

Bernard was so excited he could hardly remember how to spell his own name. But he managed it in the end.

"How'd it happen?" he asked when he'd finished.

"I fell off the school wall," said Squashy. "Can I offer you some advice, Bernard? Don't sit on the bed or the nurses go loco."

Bernard sat on a chair.

"You fell off the school wall?" he said doubtfully.

"You don't believe me?"

"I was just wondering…"

"How I got up there? Two guys pushed me."

"Two?"

"Three," admitted Squashy.

"Does it hurt?"

"It's not the pain," said Squashy. "Pain has never bothered me. It's the neighbours from hell who are getting me down."

He flicked his eyes to the left as he spoke and Bernard saw a kid of about two or three sitting up in bed clutching a plastic train.

"He keeps throwing things at me," said Squashy.

Even as he spoke the plastic train bounced off his head.

"See what I mean?"

"Why don't you tell the nurses?"

"I don't want to disturb them. They might

be having their coffee break. In any case, he's nothing in comparison with her over there."

In the bed opposite, Bernard saw a little girl of about four wearing pigtails. She smiled when she saw Bernard looking at her.

"Hello, little boy," she said. "My name is Trudy. What's yours?"

"Whatever you do, don't speak to her," said Squashy. "That's the Golden Rule round here. Otherwise, she'll tell you about her wabbit."

"Wabbit?" said Bernard.

"Wabbit," said Squashy.

"I'm talking to you, little boy," said a voice.

"Why does she call me little boy?" asked Bernard.

"Because she's round the bend."

A cloth book landed with a flappy noise on Squashy's chest.

"Don't say anything," he said. "If you do, he'll probably throw his bed." A tractor hit him. "If my mother doesn't hurry I could end up seriously dead."

"People don't usually die in hospital," Bernard said cheerily.

"If you want my personal opinion, Bernard," said Squashy, "more people die in this hospital than anywhere else in the known universe."

"My daddy reads a book to me every night," Trudy told them.

"You'd think if you'd broken your leg they'd show you some mercy instead of sticking you among a bunch of kids," said Squashy.

"Is your leg broken as well?" asked Bernard.

"The ankle is part of the leg, Bernard," Squashy explained. "You'd know that if you'd reached Purple Level Two."

"I have a white fluffy bunny wabbit," Trudy said.

"What did I tell you?" said Squashy as a ball bounced off his head.

"When's your mum coming?"

"If I'm lucky she might have started putting on her face. Have you finished those badges?"

"Badges?"

Squashy leaned forward and whispered, "Our secret club badges."

"Why are you whispering?" asked Trudy.

"Oh, those badges!" said Bernard. "I'd nearly forgotten them."

"It's rude to whisper," Trudy told them.

"Actually," said Bernard, "I've finished them."

"Doog," said Squashy. "Very doog indeed."

"Why are you saying funny words?" asked Trudy.

"I thought maybe we should change the name?" said Bernard.

"Nodrap?"

"Maybe we should call it The Triangle Gang."

"Nodrap? Nodrap?"

"Then we could have Ozzie in as well."

"You've got to be joking! It was Ozzie who got the others to shove me up the wall. If I hadn't gone up the wall I couldn't have fell off. My mother says if I speak to him once more she'll sell the dog."

Something big, red and dangerous just missed Bernard.

"Anyhow," he said standing up but keeping his head down, "maybe I better be going. I don't want to be late for dinner."

"Doog idea," said Squashy. "Very doog. If you happen to see my mother tell her not to bother to come now because it's already too late. Tell her I've died of starvation or something. And thanks for coming, Bernard. You're a real pal."

"Oireech," said Bernard, smiling.

And Squashy said "Oireech" as well.

Chapter 10

All the way to school Bernard was determined to say no, even when he was feeling in his pocket to make sure the two pounds were still there.

At dinner-time he asked for extra beans and the dinner lady said, "Not like you, Bernard! Fancy an extra sausage as well?"

Bernard shook his head because while extra beans might help calm his tummy an extra sausage could overdo things.

Take the first step, Bernard, he told himself as he finished off his banana yoghurt, and straight after dinner he went to the Boys' toilet. It was empty when he went in. *Learn to say no!* he said as he checked the coins again but he almost fainted when Baxter walked in.

"Where's my money?" asked Baxter and before Bernard knew what was happening he had handed the two pounds over.

"You got any more on you?"

Bernard actually had ten pence change from his dinner money. But he didn't say anything.

"I'm asking you a question!" said Baxter.

"No," said Bernard.

One small step, he thought.

"You sure?" Baxter seized hold of his shoulder and pulled back his fist, just as he had when he'd slammed the cubicle door. Bernard was never quite sure what would have happened next. He was wondering whether to say no or save his good looks when Ozzie came in.

"What's up?" Ozzie asked.

He seemed to know at once what was happening.

"Nothing," said Baxter.

"You pushing my friend around?" said Ozzie.

"Go play somewhere else, Ozzie. I don't want to spoil your face."

"Sez who?" said Ozzie. He went close to Baxter and grinned up at him with his loopy grin.

"Cool down," said Baxter. By now he had let go of Bernard. "This kid owes me money."

Ozzie looked at Bernard. Then he looked back at Baxter.

"He says he doesn't owe you anything," he said.

Bernard was amazed because as far as he knew, he hadn't spoken.

Baxter stared down at Ozzie. If he had poked out his fist he would have hit Ozzie smack on the nose.

But for some reason he didn't.

"OK," he said. "If that's the way you want it, Ozzie…"

Baxter started to move away.

"Just a tick." Ozzie looked back at Bernard. "He squeeze some money out of you, Bernard?"

Bernard managed a pale smile.

"How much?"

Bernard couldn't speak.

Ozzie turned to Baxter and said, "Give him it back!"

"What?"

"You heard!"

"I'll flatten you in a minute, Ozzie!" said Baxter.

"Sez who?" said Ozzie again. He went right up to Baxter and grinned up at his face. Loopy-loopy. For some reason this seemed to persuade Baxter because he gave Ozzie the two pounds. Ozzie passed them to Bernard. "OK?"

Bernard tried to smile.

"He owe you anything else?" Ozzie asked.

Bernard tried to say yes but couldn't manage it.

"How much?" said Ozzie. Bernard opened and shut his mouth but no sound came out.

Ozzie turned back to Baxter.

"How much else you taken from my friend?"

"Nothing."

"Twenty-seven p!" croaked Bernard.

Another small step!

"Hand it over!" said Ozzie.

"I haven't got it on me," said Baxter.

"You better have!"

Baxter took a lot of change out of his pocket.

"I don't have the right change," he said. "I've only got thirty pence."

"That'll do!" said Ozzie.

"Something up, Bernard?" Ozzie asked when Baxter had gone. "You look pale. Maybe you need one of your pills."

"I'll be OK," said Bernard.

But he leaned on one of the wash-basins, just in case.

Ozzie gave him the thirty pence.

"Thanks a lot, Ozzie."

Ozzie smiled. "Once a pal, always a pal," he said.

Bernard tried hard to smile, though he knew what was coming next.

Ozzie held out his hands to be slapped: Bernard slapped them as gently as he could. Then he held out his own hands and Ozzie gave him an absolute whammer. Bernard tried not to cry.

Ozzie stepped up to the urinal.

"You brought your pet, Bernard?"

It was some moments before Bernard could speak.

"I haven't really got one," he managed to say.

"Tough. I'll give you one of Oscar's babies when he has them."

"Thanks," said Bernard smiling. The idea of being given one of Oscar's babies gave him the creeps but on the whole it didn't seem likely. "And thanks a lot for getting my money back as well."

"Baxter is a big bag of wind," said Ozzie.

"But I saw him punch a door. He does karate."

"No kidding?" said Ozzie, grinning as he stepped down. "Watch this, Bernard."

He went towards the cubicle door and pulled it towards him exactly as Baxter had done.

"Watching?" He pulled his fist back *slam!* Straight into the door. The door flew back

and bounced off the side wall *bang!* Ozzie
grinned and held out his fist. It was
unmarked.

Bernard was amazed. "Do you do karate as
well?" he asked.

"No, I do turnips," said Ozzie.

It took Bernard some time to get the joke.

"It's a trick, Bernard," said Ozzie. "Watch.
You kick it with your boot. You don't touch it
with your fist. Anybody can do it." He did it
again. *Slam-bang!* "Gerrit?"

"Gorrit," said Bernard.

Ozzie grinned and went out.

After he'd gone Bernard tried the trick
himself but something must have gone
wrong. He missed the door with his boot and
hit it with his ankle instead.

It was some time before he could walk.

Chapter 11

When Bernard went into the classroom everybody was gathered round Ozzie, who was letting Oscar run round his head. All the girls were screaming and all the boys were laughing to pretend they weren't scared.

"Shall we all sit down now?" Miss Trim said.

"Can I keep Oscar on my head, Miss?" asked Ozzie.

"I don't really think that's a good idea, Oswald," said Miss Trim.

"Oscar might catch fleas, Miss!" Edward Wallboy shouted.

"Miss, can I let him go on the floor?" Elaine Goody screamed.

"Back in his box this moment, please, Oswald. Thank you so much. Now, this morning what did we decide pets were *not* for?

"Christmas, Miss," said Elaine Goody.

"Yes, Elaine. Pets are not just for Christmas. What *are* they for?"

"Pancake Tuesday, Miss!" said Edward Wallboy.

Miss Trim ignored him.

"Life, Miss," said Elaine Goody.

"Well done again, Elaine!" said Miss Trim. "Now, in a moment I'm going to ask you to write about your pets, but first perhaps I could tell you a few things about mine. He's a cat, nine years old, and I call him Octo. I wonder if anybody knows why?"

"Because he's a *puss*, Miss!" said Elaine Goody, giggling.

It was obviously meant to be some kind of joke because everybody laughed. Bernard was trying to work it out when his mind started wandering. He was remembering the time when they lost Emily Poot, then found her in the coal scuttle, all black. Then he realized Miss Trim was close to him.

"Well, Bernard?" she was asking.

She had obviously asked him a question but what the question was Bernard hadn't a clue.

"He hasn't got one, Miss," said Ozzie. "He told me in the bogs."

Miss Trim gave him a look because you weren't allowed to say *bogs*.

"Thank you for that rudeness, Oswald," she said. "So you haven't a pet, Bernard?"

"He's telling lies, Miss," said Debra Doakes. "He's got a dog."

"I'm sure Bernard would never tell a lie."

"He has, Miss!" said Shaleen. "I've seen it in the park!"

Shaleen was Debra's best friend. Last Christmas they'd both worn their mothers' high heels at the disco and been sent home by Mr Fearby in case they broke their legs.

"It's a sausage dog, Miss," said Debra. "Called Cheri."

"Miss," said Louise. "Cheri is really his mum's dog, so she doesn't count."

"Our dog doesn't count as well, Miss!" said Edward Wallboy.

Everybody laughed.

"He can lend Oscar tonight, Miss, if he wants," said Ozzie.

"How very kind, Oswald! Would you like to

borrow Oscar, Bernard?"

Bernard didn't know what to say. The idea of Oscar roaming about the house was enough to give him nightmares.

"He's scared, Miss!" said Edward Wallboy.

"Miss, Cheri might eat Oscar if she gets hungry," said Louise.

"Good thinking, Louise!" said Miss Trim. "Perhaps it's not such a good idea after all."

When they had to write about their pets Bernard decided to write about Emily Poot. He'd been thinking a lot about her lately. All the funny things she used to do. The way her whiskers twitched.

He copied the title from the board and wrote: *my pet was emily poot she was very nice*, then wondered what he could write next. He looked round and saw Ozzie winking at him, so he winked back. *Once a pal, always a pal.* When Miss Trim told them to stop writing he found he had written nearly fifteen words (he was halfway through a word when she told them to stop). That was a record!

He was packing his things away in his bag when Louise came up to him and said, "I'm sorry you haven't a special pet of your own, Bernard. I wondered if you'd like one of mine?" She held a matchbox towards him. "Mine's just had babies."

Until that moment Bernard had always admired Louise Bruce, and not just because she was kind, had eyes like a mouse and was on Purple Level Six. But did she seriously believe that matchboxes had babies? Then he realized there must be something inside the box.

"Thanks a lot, Louise," he said as he took it.

"Aren't you going to open it?" she asked.

"Not just now," he said. "I think I'll open it later."

Chapter 12

Bernard thought about opening Louise's matchbox later that night when he was up in his bedroom getting ready to go out with his mum and Tony to the Taj Mahal. But he decided to put it off just a little longer.

In any case, Tony would soon be arriving to pick them up. Mr Ravi would probably give them the table next to the carved wooden elephant and light the candles for them because he thought Bernard was special. "How come I haven't got a son like Bernard?" he kept saying.

Mr Ravi's son was called Icky, a big beefy boy who played cricket for the local team. "How come I got a son like Icky instead of Bernard? It's not fair. What have I done wrong to deserve this?"

Bernard was sorry for him, of course, but he knew that not everybody in this world could be lucky.

His new sweatshirt looked pretty good. He'd had to spend all his dad's money but he still wasn't sorry. It made him look tough.

Maybe one day he would be tough. Maybe one day he'd be able to look loopily up at big boys who tried to push him around. Maybe one day he'd be able to bang the toilet door back against the wall. In the meantime his ankle was still hurting. So maybe he wasn't so tough just yet.

There was one thing he could do, though. Another small step.

The reason he hadn't yet opened Louise's matchbox was that he was scared about what might be inside. But suddenly he wasn't scared any longer. Maybe that was because of his new sweatshirt.

Just as he was beginning to open the box, he heard Tony's car coming down their street. He waited till Tony was in the house before he pushed it open a bit more.

At first he thought it was a twig in there. He wondered if Louise had played a trick on him. But that didn't seem likely. Louise was too nice a girl to play tricks. He pushed the box open even further – *another* small step –

and now he could see what it was. A twig insect! He should have known! Or was it a stick insect? Yes, that was it! He opened the matchbox fully.

The stick insect didn't move. Bernard liked that. "Hello, Stick Insect?" he said. The stick insect didn't reply but Bernard felt it was listening. In a way he couldn't think of anything nicer a person could have given him. It seemed the perfect pet. It would be unlikely to get killed on the road, and he could even keep it in his trouser pocket – like Ozzie kept Oscar – as long as he was careful. He wondered whether he should call it Sticky or Twiglet.

One thing was certain. He had a pet now. His own real personal pet. A friend for life. Because that's what a pet was.

He was glad Louise had given it to him. It was funny how she always did the right thing. She was another true friend.

And maybe they weren't the only ones. He thought of Ozzie. *Once a pal, always a pal.* And

Squashy. And Dr Tom and the two nurses who'd remembered him. And, now he came to think of it, there was Mr Ravi and Miss Trim. Maybe he could even count the dinner lady who'd offered him an extra sausage.

Really he had a lot more friends than he'd ever imagined. Maybe more than anybody else in the known universe. They were like a kind of gang. *His* gang.

And there was still one he hadn't counted.

Just thinking of Louise had somehow reminded him of Emily Poot. He could feel her presence now. Definitely. She was definitely in the room. Maybe she had seen him after all as he'd looked down from the landing window.

"You ready, Bernard?" his mum called from downstairs.

"Last one down pays the bill!" said Tony.

"Sez who?" said Bernard, smiling to himself.

Then he went downstairs to join them.